Dedication

I give GOD all the glory and honor for giving me His GOD-given energy, creativity and wisdom. I thank Him for sending me Tahitian Noni Juice to be used as a vessel for helping me do His great works. It boosted my energy and kept me focused. I thank my beautiful wife, Vicky for pushing me also to get this book published. I thank my beautiful kids, Jami, Travis, and Sean for inspiring me to be a better father for them. I especially thank my brothers Derrick W. Jones, David E. Jones, III, and sister Felissia V. (Jones) Thomas for inspiring my writing children's stories. I want to also thank Marion Nelson, of First Page Publications in Livonia, MI (2004), for her help. May God bless her and her family, wherever they may live.

I want to give a shout-out thank you to my church family, the Open Door Church Of GOD In Christ, Ypsilanti, MI. My Pastor is Harris H. Johnson and First Lady Annise Johnson.

I wished that this could have been done years earlier, but, I guess it wasn't the time for my boat to float. I dreamed . . . and dreamed . . . and dreamed. I worked it . . . and worked it . . . and worked it. And, now it's a reality. Thank you, beautiful people! —Dwayne F. Jones

Layout Designer: Ranilo Cabo

To order additional copies of this book, contact:
Xlibris
844-714-8691
www.Xlibris.com
Orders@Xlibris.com

ISBN: Softcover   978-1-4257-8860-5
             Hardcover   978-1-4257-8864-3

Print information available on the last page

Rev. date: 09/08/2021

ABDUL

and the Gold-Blue Ring

WRITTEN BY Dwayne F. Jones

ILLUSTRATED BY William Alexander, III

Abdul was always complaining about something. His house was never large enough for his family. He wanted to have more food in the kitchen cupboards. Abdul did not even like anyone making decisions for him. He wanted to be in charge.

One evening, Abdul went walking by the railroad tracks near his home. He stopped at a huge rock, wiped it off, and sat on it. Feeling hungry, he grabbed bread from his pants pocket and shoved it in his mouth. The bread crumbled as Abdul bit into it.

"What a life! Bread is nothing to me. I want more! I wonder what it would be like to be a king. Kings have everything! I could eat anything that I want. I could do anything that I want, and give orders. Nobody could tell me what to do," Abdul said.

Suddenly, Abdul saw a train zipping across the old railroad tracks. Soon after, he noticed something that began glowing. Whatever it was gave off a bright blue glow.

"Now what is that?" Abdul asked himself. He slid down off the rock and walked quickly over to it.

Closer and closer he got. Right on the rusty tracks was a round thing. It was a gold ring! Abdul's eyes widened as he grinned from ear to ear. He touched it. His fingerprints were on the ring. Yes, it was actually real! Never in a million years did he think that he would ever be so fortunate. No, he was not dreaming.

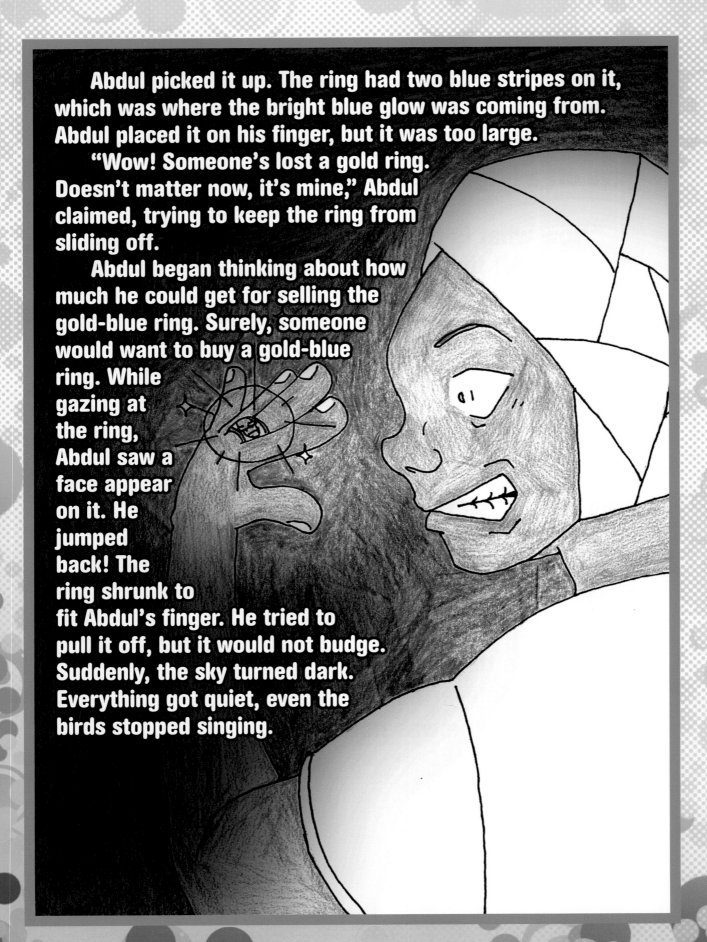

Abdul picked it up. The ring had two blue stripes on it, which was where the bright blue glow was coming from. Abdul placed it on his finger, but it was too large.

"Wow! Someone's lost a gold ring. Doesn't matter now, it's mine," Abdul claimed, trying to keep the ring from sliding off.

Abdul began thinking about how much he could get for selling the gold-blue ring. Surely, someone would want to buy a gold-blue ring. While gazing at the ring, Abdul saw a face appear on it. He jumped back! The ring shrunk to fit Abdul's finger. He tried to pull it off, but it would not budge. Suddenly, the sky turned dark. Everything got quiet, even the birds stopped singing.

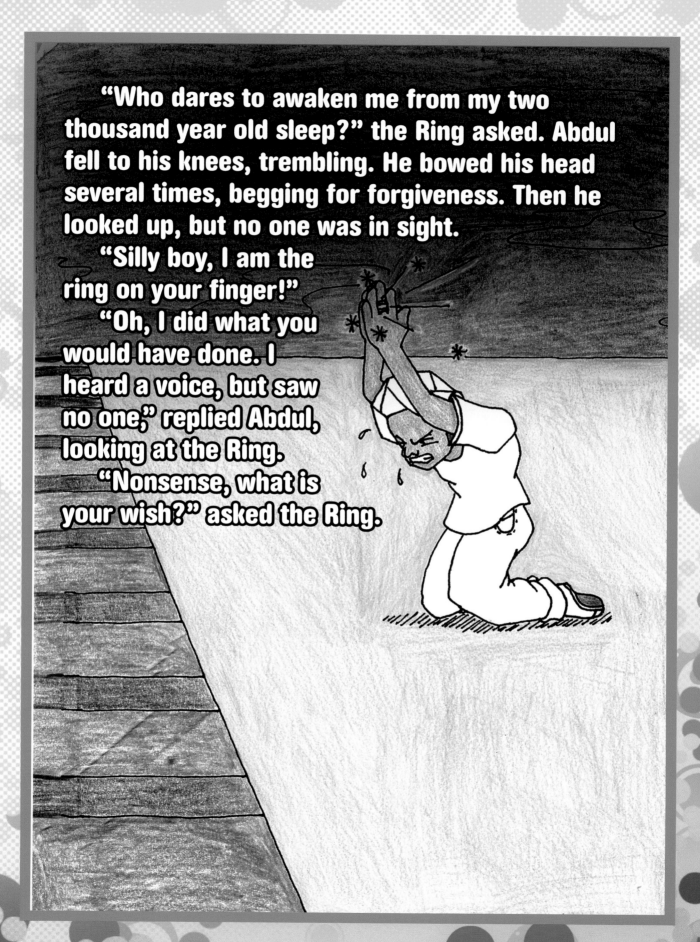

"Who dares to awaken me from my two thousand year old sleep?" the Ring asked. Abdul fell to his knees, trembling. He bowed his head several times, begging for forgiveness. Then he looked up, but no one was in sight.

"Silly boy, I am the ring on your finger!"

"Oh, I did what you would have done. I heard a voice, but saw no one," replied Abdul, looking at the Ring.

"Nonsense, what is your wish?" asked the Ring.

"You mean to tell me that you can grant wishes?" Abdul asked, noticing the bright blue glow as it talked.

"Surely, you don't think that a genie could. So, what do you wish?" asked the Ring.

Abdul pretended to be thinking. He did not rush his request. Finally, Abdul gave in by making a grumbling noise, signaling that he had come to a decision about what he wanted. The Ring sighed with relief.

"I know! I want to be a king!" Abdul said.

"Don't you want to think about it first?" asked the Ring.

"No! I want to be a king," said Abdul.

"That's the sign of a wise man. Very well, as you wish," the Ring said.

Magically, Abdul appeared upon a sparkling gold and blue throne, inside a gold and blue castle. He was a king. Blue people with big noses surrounded him. Everyone was busy quarreling.

"Bring me food, and lots of it!" Abdul commanded.
The next thing he knew, a blue cook appeared and brought him a steam surrounded gold platter with a cover. It began juggling the platter from one hand to the other.
Sweat dripped from its forehead. When the cover was lifted, Abdul's greedy face turned to a frown.

"What is this?" Abdul asked. It was a blue pig with a blue apple in its mouth. Off the platter jumped the pig and Abdul jumped from his throne and chased it.

"Taxi, oink, oink!" the pig called out.

A gold-blue taxi pulled up in a flash. The pig waved good-bye to Abdul while climbing into the taxi. Then the taxi quickly drove away.

"Lobster anyone?" asked another cook, standing beside Abdul. He lifted the lid off of his platter.

"Blue lobster?" asked Abdul, rubbing his eyes in disbelief.

"How about some bread, my king?" asked a third cook, lifting his lid.

"Blue bread? No, no, and no!
Take it away!" Abdul shouted.

"Surely, you want more. Why not make another wish?" the Ring suggested.

"Yes, I guess. What do you think?" Abdul asked, scratching his head.

"Well, how about a friend?"

"A friend, what does that have to do with being a king?"

"Are you not aware that a king always has a friend to help him rule over the kingdom? Obviously, you are not as prepared as I thought," the Ring answered.

"Okay, then give me a friend," ordered Abdul.

Poof! A lady appeared wearing a veil across her face. She was gold and blue, too. Abdul thought that she was very pretty. She started walking.

"Who is this?" Abdul asked.
The blue lady stopped next to Abdul, snatched her veil off, and smiled widely. She was missing some teeth. She grabbed Abdul's arm and began dragging him. Her hair whipped food wildly in every direction.

"That is your queen. Aren't you excited?" the Ring asked, jumping for joy on Abdul's finger.

"Queen? You said that I would be getting a friend," Abdul responded, as he pulled loose from the queen.

"Right, but, you need to have more. More of everything will make you happy!" the Ring answered.

"Well, I don't want her. And, I don't want more of her either. I want another wish," snapped Abdul.

"Very well, your loss," said the Ring. The queen instantly disappeared.

"I want gold. I want all the gold in the world."

In the blink of an eye, Abdul's pants pockets began filling with gold coins. Abdul could not move. It never dawned on him how much gold he had asked for.

The very next minute, Abdul's pants pockets began emptying, until there was nothing left.

"Ooh, what happened?" asked Abdul.

"Sorry, but you just had a reality wish," the Ring replied.
"What's a reality wish?"

"That means after a certain number of wishes, you have to pay for everything ever wished for."

"I paid for everything that I wished for?"

"You are almost right," answered the Ring. "You have just paid for the pig, the apple, the food, and the queen. Plus, you have to pay for the wishes of kids before you."

"That can't be true. I never got a chance to touch one gold coin."

"You don't have to touch anything. It happens automatically. Surely, you are not displeased?"

"I am! I am!" Abdul yelled, trying to pull the ring off his finger.

Afterwards, a group of blue businessmen approached him. There was a thin hairy man. There was a thick baldheaded man. There was a man with short legs. There was a man with long legs. There was a man with a humpback. There was even a thin hairy man with a thick baldhead with one short leg and a large leg with a humpback.

"Let's tax the poor," said the thin hairy man.

"No," replied the thick baldheaded man.

"Then we tax the rich," said the man with short legs.

"No," replied the man with long legs.

"What is taxing?" asked the man with a humpback, dumbfounded.

"I don't know. Let's ask the king. He knows! This is his wish," replied the thin hairy man with a thick baldhead, one short leg, one long leg and a humpback.

"Wait! Wait! I am too young to answer such questions," Abdul cried, burying his head in his hands.

"But, you are the king! You wanted to be a king!" answered everyone together.

"How about a nice fizzy-fizzy drink, my king?" asked a waiter. He shoved a bubbling blue drink in a gold glass at Abdul.

When Abdul saw the blue drink, he screamed and started running. He tried to pass through all the people. He dodged one here, and another one there, but they kept coming! He just could not get away. The people surrounded him again.

"I want to get out of here. This is not my wish,"
sobbed Abdul, loudly.

"You are unhappy? But, I've given you everything that you have wished for."

"Truly, I never wanted any of those things," Abdul admitted.

"Silly little boy, you are just like all the other kids. Did you really think that you would be happy with all those things? I made you a king! I gave you a kingdom with everything in it! I gave you lots of food, a queen, money, and people to rule over. I made you rich, and you were still unhappy! Listen to me, where there is gold, there is blue. Nothing comes without a price. Accept what you have and make the best of it," advised the Ring.

The bright blue glow stopped after the deep voice of the ring faded, and the gold-blue ring slid off Abdul's finger. It fell to the ground by his foot. In a second, he was back by the old rusty railroad tracks. Darkness turned back to light as the birds started singing again. Abdul thought about how many other little kids like him had worn the ring. He didn't want anyone else to experience what he had, so he picked the ring up and threw it as far as he could.

Then
he ran all
the way
home.

**Abdul hugged everyone that he lived with,
and appreciated his life from there on.**